Flying Kites

A message for grown-ups:

Sharing a Teletubbies book with your child is a wonderful way to encourage reading skills and enhance your child's development. Here are some ways Teletubbies books work for children and help their readiness to learn.

Teletubbies books:

Encourage Listening - Reading a fun story with familiar characters like the Teletubbies captivates children's attention. They will happily listen and join in.

Reinforce Speech Patterns - Teletubbies use the same words and phrases young children use, which encourages word recognition and builds their confidence.

Teach Through Repetition - Repeated pictures and text offer children comfort and pleasure in the familiar. It gives them time to think about what's happening and what's coming next.

Promote Playfulness - Teletubbies have fun! For them, everything is a game full of laughter, surprises, and funny sounds.

Build Self-esteem - Teletubbies books are full of the same affection, reassurance, and good feelings as the television program. There are plenty of Big Hugs to go around!

We hope you enjoy sharing this Teletubbies book with your child.

SCHOLASTIC INC.

New York   Toronto   London   Auckland   Sydney   Mexico City   New Delhi   Hong Kong

One day in Teletubbyland, the Teletubbies were flying their kites.

The wind blew and blew.

And then the wind stopped.

The wind blew and blew.

And then the wind stopped.

Laa-Laa wanted to play with her ball.
So she gave her kite to Dipsy to hold.

The wind blew and blew and blew.

And then the wind stopped.

The wind blew again.

And then the wind stopped.

Dipsy wanted to play with Laa-Laa.
So he gave his kites to Tinky Winky to hold.

The wind blew and blew.

And then the wind stopped.

Tinky Winky wanted to play with Dipsy and Laa-Laa.

Tinky Winky play.

So he gave his kites to Po to hold.

The wind blew and blew.

And the wind blew and blew
very hard indeed.

Po went up and up and up.

The other Teletubbies couldn't believe that Po was up, up, up in the sky.

But then Po began to go
down and down . . .

... and down.

Everyone was very happy to see Po back down again because the Teletubbies love Po very much.

Big Hug!

Look for these other storybooks:

ISBN 0-439-13856-6

From the original TV scripts by Andrew Davenport. Text, design, and illustrations: copyright 2000 Ragdoll Productions (UK) Ltd.
TELETUBBIES characters and logo: TM and © 2000 Ragdoll Productions (UK) Ltd. Licensed by The itsy bitsy Entertainment Company. All rights reserved.
Published by Scholastic Inc. SCHOLASTIC and associated logos are trademarks and/or registered trademarks of Scholastic Inc.

12 11 10 9 8 7 6 5 4 3 2 1   0/0 1/0 2/0 3/0 4/0

Printed in the U.S.A.

First Scholastic printing, April 2000